DETECTIVE MOLE
and the Tip-Top Mystery

story and pictures by
ROBERT QUACKENBUSH

Lothrop, Lee & Shepard Company
A Division of William Morrow & Company, Inc.
New York

FOR
PIET

JY
QUA
c. 2

4/79

Library of Congress Cataloging in Publication Data
Quackenbush, Robert M.
    Detective Mole and the Tip-Top mystery.
    (A fun-to-read book)
    SUMMARY: When mysterious mishaps drive guests
away from the Tip-Top Inn, Detective Mole investigates.
    [1. Mystery and detective stories. 2. Animals—
Fiction]   I. Title.
PZ7.Q16Di   [E]   78-6082
ISBN 0-688-41858-9
ISBN 0-688-51858-3 lib. bdg.

Printed in the United States of America.

First Edition
1   2   3   4   5   6   7   8   9   10

CONTENTS

1
TROUBLE AT THE INN

Detective Mole got off the bus
at Tip-Top Notch.

Emery Eagle, the manager of the
Tip-Top Inn, was waiting.

"I'm so glad you have come to
help us, Detective," he said.

Emery Eagle took Detective
Mole's briefcase and put it in
the trunk of the oldest car
Detective Mole had ever seen.

"Are you sure my briefcase will
be safe?" asked Detective
Mole. "It contains equipment
that may be important to the
solving of the case."

"Oh, yes, I think it will be
safe," said Emery Eagle, as
he cranked the car to start
it. "Though lately, I can't
be sure of anything! No one
knows what is happening to
Tip-Top."

"That is what I am here to
find out," said Detective
Mole.

The car turned through a gate
marked PRIVATE and started up
a long, winding road.
"Tell me more about the
trouble," said Detective Mole.
"Mr. and Mrs. Goat were too
upset to say much when they
phoned and asked me to come."

"All kinds of things go wrong," said Emery Eagle. "Lights go out and candles can't be found. There is salt in the sugarbowl and sugar in the saltcellars. Guests put their feet through holes in the sheets. That is, they did when we had guests. Mr. and Mrs. Pig are the only ones left!"

Suddenly the car went over a bridge and past a waterfall.

"Drip-Drop," said Emery Eagle.

"Excuse me?" said Detective Mole.

GUEST
PARKING

"Drip-Drop Falls," Emery Eagle explained. "They pour into Lake Bucket. This is beautiful and historic land. The Goat Family has owned it for two hundred years. Legend has it that there is buried treasure somewhere on the grounds."

"Hmmm," said Detective Mole.

Just then Tip-Top Inn came into view.

Mr. and Mrs. Goat were on the veranda, shouting and waving.

"Oh, dear," said Emery Eagle, "what has happened now?"

2

THE ELEVATOR BREAKDOWN

Emery Eagle and Detective Mole
hopped out of the car.

"Quick!" cried Mr. and Mrs.
Goat. "It's the elevator!
It's stuck between the third
and fourth floors. Mr. and
Mrs. Pig are inside!"

"Oh, no!" said Emery Eagle. "I
hope they aren't too upset. If
they go we won't have ANY guests."

"Let's try to keep cool," said
Detective Mole. "The first thing
is to get Mr. and Mrs. Pig out
of the elevator. Then I will
get right on the case."
Detective Mole and Emery Eagle
ran through the lobby and up
three flights of stairs to
the fourth floor.
They pried open the doors to
the elevator shaft.
They could see the top of the
elevator.
Inside, Mr. and Mrs. Pig
were pounding and shouting.

"Keep calm," called Emery
Eagle. "Help is on the way."
Detective Mole and Emery Eagle
opened a small trap door in
the ceiling of the elevator.
Looking down through it, they
could see Mr. and Mrs. Pig
shivering in their wet
bathing suits.

"Did you have a nice dip in Lake
Bucket?" asked Emery Eagle.
"Never mind that now!" shouted
Mr. Pig. "Just get us out of
here!"

Detective Mole and Emery Eagle
pulled first Mrs. Pig, then Mr.
Pig, through the tiny trap door.
"This is the worst vacation we
have ever had!" Mr. Pig shouted.
"Come, dear," said Mrs. Pig,
"you'll catch cold. I'll run a
nice hot bath. We can yell at
them later."
The Pigs went to their room.
"Now," said Detective Mole,
"let's get to the bottom of this."
Detective Mole and Emery Eagle
ran down four flights of stairs
to the basement.

When they got to the basement,
Emery Eagle borrowed Detective
Mole's flashlight.
"There," said Emery Eagle,
holding up the flashlight,
"that is the switch that makes
the elevator run."

Detective Mole looked at the
switch.

"Ah, ha!" he said. "Someone has
turned the switch to OFF!"

Detective Mole took a jar of
white powder out of his
briefcase and dusted the switch.

"What are you doing?" asked
Emery Eagle.

"Looking for telltale prints,"
answered Detective Mole. "But
there don't seem to be any.

Whoever has done this has wiped
the switch clean!"

3

THE QUESTIONING

As soon as the elevator was
running again, Emery Eagle
showed Detective Mole up to
his room.

"While I unpack," said Detective
Mole, "would you please ask the
hotel staff to gather in the
lobby? I would like to meet
them and ask a few questions.
I will be down in a moment."

Detective Mole unpacked his
toothbrush, his pajamas,
and his sleep shades.
Then he went into the bathroom
to wash his face and paws.
He turned on the faucet.

First the water was very,
very hot.

Next it was very, very cold.

Then there was no water at all.

"Hmmm," said Detective Mole.

"I bet someone has just shut off
the main water pipe. If I hurry,
I might catch the culprit."

Detective Mole grabbed his
briefcase and jumped into the
elevator.

He rode down to the basement.

No one was there.

But sure enough, someone had
shut off the water.

Detective Mole took out his
white powder.
Again, there were no prints.
Detective Mole turned the water
back on.

Suddenly he remembered Mr. and
Mrs. Pig, and the hot bath they
had been about to take.

"Uh-oh," Detective Mole thought,
"I had better go and warn Emery
Eagle. There may be a fuss."
Detective Mole ran up to the
lobby.

But Mr. and Mrs. Pig were
already there.

They were wearing their bathrobes
and carrying their suitcases.

"This is the last straw!" Mr.
Pig shouted. "Give us our bill
so we can refuse to pay it!"

Detective Mole ran forward.
"Please don't go yet, Mr. and Mrs.
Pig," he said. "The water
is back on. I am a detective.
I am about to hold a meeting,
and I would like you to stay."

"Yes, do sit down and join us,"
said Mr. Goat. "Detective Mole
will get to the bottom of things."
"This IS the bottom," said Mr.
Pig. "This place should be
called the Rock-Bottom Inn.
But since our vacation is
ruined, we may as well stay."
Mr. and Mrs. Pig sat down.
Emery Eagle introduced the rest
of the staff to Detective Mole.
There was Ms. Cockatoo, who did
the linens, the Pelican sisters,
who cooked, and Otto Otter, the
lifeguard at Lake Bucket.

"How did those holes get in the sheets, Ms. Cockatoo?" Detective Mole asked suddenly.

"Why, I don't know," Ms. Cockatoo answered. "I don't know how the roof of the linen closet caved in this morning, either. There won't be any clean towels for quite some time."

Mr. and Mrs. Pig groaned.
Detective Mole turned to the
Pelican sisters.
"How did the salt get in the
sugarbowls?" he asked them.
"Ask Emery Eagle," the Pelican
sisters said. "He waits on the
tables. We stay in the kitchen
and mind our own business."

"If your business is cooking,
you don't mind it very well,"
said Mrs. Pig. "The food is
dreadful. I bet you switched
the salt and sugar yourselves,
to keep us from noticing what
bad cooks you are."

"Hmmm," said Detective Mole.
He turned to Otto Otter.
"How come nothing has gone
wrong at Lake Bucket?" he asked.
"Something did, just last night,"
Otto Otter replied. "Someone
broke into the boat house."

"Hmmm," said Detective Mole.

"I will go check it out. But
first I would like to talk in
private with Mr. and Mrs. Goat.
Mr. Eagle, please stay, too.
The rest of you may go back
to what you were doing."
"I hope so," said Mr. Pig.

4
THE LOST TREASURE

When the staff and guests were gone, Detective Mole turned to Mr. and Mrs. Goat.

"There is something you should know," he said. "Someone is trying to force you to close the Tip-Top Inn. I think I know why. Mr. Eagle has given me a clue."

"He has?" said Emery Eagle with surprise. "What is it?"

"You mentioned a legend of buried treasure," said Detective Mole. "I think that a crook or crooks are after that treasure. If Tip-Top were empty, they could hunt for it with much less risk of being caught. So they are causing trouble to drive the guests away."

"It looks as if their plan might work," said Mrs. Goat. "We can't keep Tip-Top open at this rate!"

"Tell me more about the treasure," said Detective Mole.

"The legend says it was buried
by Silas Goat," Mr. Goat said.
"Silas was an innkeeper in the
Old Country. He came here to
set up the first inn in the
New Land. That was two hundred
years ago."

"I see," said Detective Mole.
"Please go on, Mr. Goat."

"Well," Mr. Goat continued,
"on Silas Goat's first trip to
the New Land, all he could
bring over was silver:
silver dishes, candlesticks,
knives, forks, and spoons. He
went back to the Old Country
to fetch furniture and linens,
burying the silver here for
safekeeping while he was gone.
But his ship was lost at sea,
and Silas never returned. His
brother and sister came and
took over, and carried out his
dream of founding Tip-Top."

"And the brother and sister
never found the treasure?"
said Detective Mole.

"No," said Mr. Goat, "they
never found the silver, or
the map that showed where
it was buried."

"A map?" said Detective Mole.

"Yes," said Mrs. Goat. "Silas
hid a map, probably somewhere
by Lake Bucket. What is now
the boat house was once Silas's
cabin."

"Hmmm," said Detective Mole,
"I think it is time to go
check out the boat house.
Would you show me the way,
please, Mr. Eagle?"

5

THE TELLTALE PRINTS

Emery Eagle led Detective Mole
down to Lake Bucket.
"Here is the boat house,"
Emery Eagle said.
But Detective Mole was busy
looking at the ground through
his magnifying glass.
"Ah, ha!" he said. "Footprints
in the mud! Some telltale
evidence at last!"

"Couldn't those be Otto Otter's prints?" asked Emery Eagle.

"I don't think so," Detective Mole said. "Otto Otter has webbed feet. These prints look different. But I'll make a cast of them to be sure."

Detective Mole mixed some plaster and poured it into the prints.

He waited a few minutes for the plaster to harden.

Then he pulled up perfect copies of the prints.

"I have never seen anyone at
the Inn with feet like that,"
said Emery Eagle.

"Well, I have seen prints like
these before," said Detective
Mole, "but I can't at the
moment remember where. When
we get back to the Inn I will
look them up in my detective
manual. But now I will go
check things out in the boat
house."

Detective Mole went into the
boat house.
Suddenly there was a
tremendous crash!
"Detective Mole!" cried Emery
Eagle, "Are you all right!
Where are you?"
"Down here," said Detective
Mole, "a floorboard gave way.
But I've spotted something. Get
a rope and pull me up."
Emery Eagle got a rope from
one of the boats and tossed
one end down to Detective Mole.

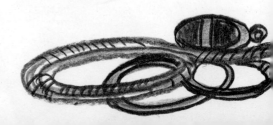

Emery Eagle pulled Detective
Mole up to safety.

Detective Mole held something
up for Emery Eagle to see.
It was an old leather pouch!
Detective Mole opened it.
He pulled out a piece
of parchment and unrolled it.
"Silas Goat's map!" cried
Emery Eagle.
"Let's see," said Detective
Mole, "X marks the spot. Hmmm.
It looks as if the treasure is
in a cave behind Drip-Drop
Falls. Lead the way, Mr. Eagle."

6

THE SECRET CAVE

Emery Eagle led Detective Mole
on a long hike through the
woods around Lake Bucket.
At last they came to the
bottom of Drip-Drop Falls.
Detective Mole took out
Silas Goat's map.
"I don't see the cave," shouted
Emery Eagle. "Do you see it,
Detective Mole?"

Detective Mole looked through
his binoculars.

"Yes," he said finally, "it's
way up there. It is a spot a
goat would choose, all right.
Only a goat could get to it!"

"I can get to it," said Emery
Eagle. "Wait here, Detective."
Emery Eagle flew up behind
the Falls.

In a few moments, he was back.
In his beak was a silver
candlestick.

"There is enough silver there
to fill a museum," Emery Eagle
said. "I brought this back to
show Mr. and Mrs. Goat."
Detective Mole put the
candlestick into Silas's pouch.
"Well done, Emery," he said.
"Now we had better hurry back
to the Inn. I have just had a
hunch about those footprints.
I think I am about to close
the case, and you can help me."

7

A TUG AT THE RUG

Back at the Inn, Detective
Mole took a quick look at his
detective manual.
"My hunch about those
footprints is right!" he said.
"Now for the proof."
Emery Eagle called everyone
to the lobby.
"Detective Mole has something
to tell you," he said.

Detective Mole stood behind a
large hooked rug and began
to speak very softly.
Soon everyone was standing on
the rug so they could hear
Detective Mole.
"Now, Emery!" Detective Mole
said suddenly.

Emery Eagle gave the rug a
sharp tug.

Everyone crashed to the floor.

"We'll sue!" cried Mr. Pig.

"Sorry, folks," said Detective
Mole in his normal voice. "It
was the only way for me to see
what I had to see. You may all
be seated now."

Everyone grumbled as they
dusted themselves off and went
to their seats.

Detective Mole held up the
plaster foot prints.

"These prints belong to the
crooks who have been trying to
close down Tip-Top," he
said. "They belong to two of
you."

The Pelican sisters got up
suddenly and tried to leave
the room.

Detective Mole was ready for
them.

"You're not going anywhere,"
he said.

He grabbed hold of the Pelican
sisters' beaks and pulled hard.

"Introducing the Raccoon
brothers," said Detective Mole,
"—two of the biggest crooks
in the country. Their prints
are published in my detective
manual. I suspected that I
might not find pelican feet
underneath those long aprons.
But the only way to get proof
was to pull the rug out from
under them!"

"We're cooks, not crooks!"
cried the Raccoon brothers.

"A jury will decide that,"
said Detective Mole.

He locked the Raccoon brothers
in the cashier's cage.
Then Detective Mole went over
to Mr. and Mrs. Goat.
He took the silver candlestick
out of the leather pouch.

"Silas Goat's treasure has been
found," Detective Mole said,
"and this is just a sample.
There is enough old silver to
fill a museum. When the news is
out, guests will come from all
over to see historic Tip-Top!"
Mr. and Mrs. Goat were speechless.
"May I take a look at that?" said
Mr. Pig. "I am an antique dealer."

Detective Mole handed him the candlestick.

"Why, this is indeed a priceless heirloom," Mr. Pig said to Mr. and Mrs. Goat. "I would be happy to stay on at the Inn and help you declare the value of your treasure."

"HOORAY!" everyone shouted.

Mr. and Mrs. Goat finally found their voices.

"Detective Mole," they said, "you have saved Tip-Top Inn. How can we ever thank you?"

"All in a day's work," said
Detective Mole modestly. "No
need for thanks. But there is
something you can do for me.
Let me cook for the Inn
until you hire a new chef.
Cooking is my favorite
hobby."

"Why, that would be Tip-Top!"
said Mrs. Goat. "What's for
lunch?"

"Banana Crunch à la Mole,"
said Detective Mole, "my
specialty!"

Detective Mole's

BANANA CRUNCH

12 graham crackers
8-ounce package cream cheese
3 bananas

1. Break graham crackers in half.
2. Spread 12 cracker halves with cream cheese and set aside.
3. Slice bananas and place 4 slices on each of the remaining cracker halves.
4. Put cheese halves, cheese side down, on top of banana halves.
5. Sprinkle with powdered sugar, if desired, and serve. Serves 6.

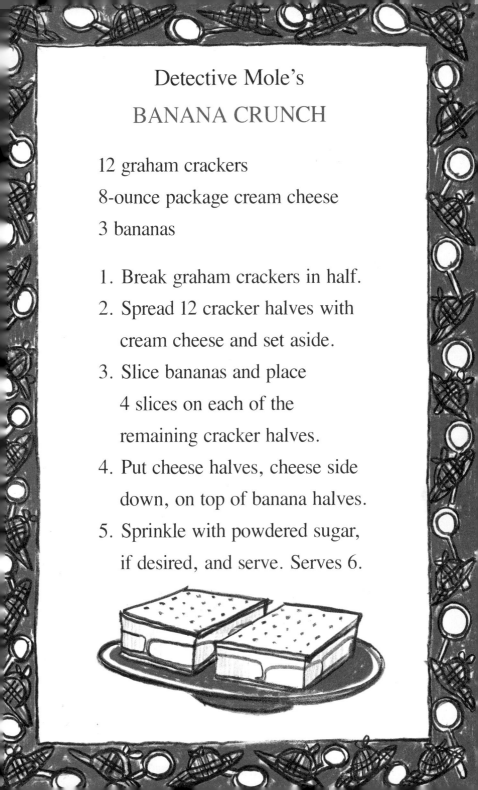

ROBERT QUACKENBUSH, an outstanding author/illustrator of children's books, lives in New York City with his wife and son. The Quackenbushes have vacationed at a mountain resort not far from Tip-Top.

Other Fun-to-Read books by
Robert Quackenbush

ANIMAL CRACKS
CALLING DOCTOR QUACK
DETECTIVE MOLE
DETECTIVE MOLE
   And The Secret Clues
MR. SNOW BUNTING'S SECRET
PETE PACK RAT
PETE PACK RAT
   And The Gila Monster Gang
SHERIFF SALLY GOPHER
   And The Haunted Dance Hall